Lori Weber

Fitzhenry & Whiteside

Published in Canada by Fitzhenry & Whiteside, 195 Allstate Parkway, Markham, Ontario L3R 4T8

Published in the United States by Fitzhenry & Whiteside, 311 Washington Street, Brighton, Massachusetts 02135

www.fitzhenry.ca   godwit@fitzhenry.ca

10 9 8 7 6 5 4 3 2 1

Library and Archives Canada Cataloguing in Publication
Weber, Lori, 1959-
    Yellow mini / Lori Weber.
ISBN 978-1-55455-199-6
    I. Title.
PS8645.E24Y44 2011   jC813'.6   C2011-905599-6

Publisher Cataloging-in-Publication Data (U.S)
 Weber, Lori, 1959-
    Yellow mini / Lori Weber.
[248] p. : cm.
Summary: A powerful free-verse novel that intertwines the coming-of-age stories of five teens and their relationships with each other, their parents, and themselves.
ISBN: 978-1-55455-199-6 (pbk.)
1. Teenagers – Juvenile fiction. 2. Parent and teenager – Juvenile fiction. I. Title.
[F] dc22   PZ7.W4347Ye   2011

Fitzhenry & Whiteside acknowledges with thanks the Canada Council for the Arts, and the Ontario Arts Council for their support of our publishing program. We acknowledge the financial support of the Government of Canada through the Canada Book Fund for our publishing activities.

ONTARIO ARTS COUNCIL
CONSEIL DES ARTS DE L'ONTARIO

Canada Council   Conseil des Arts
for the Arts   du Canada

Cover and interior design by Daniel Choi
Cover image courtesy Christie Harkin
Printed in Canada

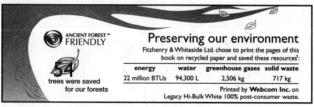

ANCIENT FOREST™
FRIENDLY

Preserving our environment
Fitzhenry & Whiteside Ltd. chose to print the pages of this book on recycled paper and saved these resources[1]:

energy	water	greenhouse gases	solid waste
22 million BTUs	94,300 L	2,506 kg	717 kg

54
trees were saved
for our forests

Printed by **Webcom Inc.** on
Legacy Hi-Bulk White 100% post-consumer waste.

[1]Estimates were made using the Environmental Defense Paper Calculator.

98 %

FSC
www.fsc.org

MIX

Paper from
responsible sources

FSC® C004071

Dedication:

For Fran, cherished friend, teacher, and mentor, who first taught
me to believe all those years ago.

Acknowledgements::

A huge thank you to Cassandra Curtis, Ron Curtis, and Jane Barclay who read my tangled web of poems with great insight and gave me invaluable advice. Thanks to Fran Davis who listened to an early draft over tea and then never stopped asking. Thanks also to my editor, Christie Harkin, for falling for the book and then helping me take it to a higher level. Thanks also to the design team at Fitzhenry & Whiteside for their creativity. Thank you to the Canada Council for the financial support that enabled me to write this book. Finally, thanks to two special cats, Silver and Bogart, who keep me amused while writing, which is more important than I can say.

The Third Floor

Annabelle

I hate to walk past the third floor lounge
      of my school, where
      the cool kids
      hang out.

The cool kids talk loud and dress preppy,
      carry condoms in their pencil
      cases and smoke up at
      break, throwing
      their butts
      into the
      bushes.

If I have to go to the library, I take the second floor
      as far as it will go, then climb
      the stairs and double
      back, just to avoid
      the third floor
      lounge.

If I really can't avoid it, I hold my head so high I get a kink
        in my neck, and I try not to look anyone straight
        in the eyes, because if they know you're
        looking they flaunt it, their
        popularity, pull it out
        of tight tops like a
        magician's scarf
        and fling it,
        laughing,
        in your
        face.

My ex-best friend Stacey hangs out there with
        her boyfriend Mark, wrapping him
        around her like a shawl, the hair
        on his head spiked up
        with gel to make
        him look
        taller.

If Stacey sees me, she'll wave and holler, *Hey Annabelle, how's it going?*
        and even though she doesn't say it, I know she means
        down here, among the loser girls who haven't done
        it yet, girls who think the purpose of school is
        getting good marks and not a boyfriend
        named Mark, who drives a yellow
        Mini, his girl of the month
        beaming beside him
        like a yellow car
        Princess.

Crossed Over
Stacey

Sometimes, I want to pull
her in and give her
a makeover.

It wouldn't be hard—
she's not ugly.

She's got amazing green eyes,
thick brown hair,
and a decent shape,
not that you'd know it because
she hides herself under
peasant skirts and baggy shirts.

Sometimes, I think of the olden days
when we'd sit on my bed, eat chips
and talk about the third floor gang,
wondering if we'd ever be one of them.

Sometimes, I can't believe I crossed over,
all because I learned how to flirt with guys
on holiday at a cottage my parents rented
last summer by a lake.

There, I met Paul, who could skip rocks
ten bobs on the water. He said when he
saw me his heart exploded.

We kissed on the big rock, way out
in the middle of the lake, our tongues

sparking like flint. With each spark,
a piece of my childhood chipped
and fell into the lake, taking away
the geeky girl I had been.

My parents were tiny as paper dolls
in their beach chairs, noses in their books,
and by the time I was back on shore
I knew I'd leave them
and Annabelle behind.

Now, in the third floor lounge, Mark and I
entwine under the florescent lights
and I shine—*his* girl, not loser girl
with Annabelle and Mary anymore.

Now, I'm the girl who gets to hang her arm
out the yellow Mini and wave
at suckers waiting for buses.

I get to roll with Mark beside me,
his left hand on the steering wheel,
his right hand on my thigh.

The way he speeds through stop signs
makes my blood race and I want to keep
driving forever, leaving school further
and further behind because I can't see
how it's going to give me what Mark
gives me, which is the feeling that
I'm someone who's going somewhere

fast.

The Kind of Life I Want
Annabelle

My mom's had to work hard
because she's a *single* mom.

That term always makes me imagine
that other people have *double* moms
or *triple* moms—a *string* of moms
stuck together like those paper cut-outs
we used to make in kindergarten.

My mom says she's a *woman surviving in a man's world,*
which means she has to be careful about how she dresses
and acts at work, where mostly *men* get promoted.

She wears two-piece suits and pointy-toed shoes,
and carries a leather briefcase full of stats
on house sales, interest rates, and mortgages.

She smiles at meetings while the men crack dirty jokes
and loosen their ties because *they* can let their hair down,
while *hers* has to be impeccably cut and streaked.

My mom says it's a *disgrace* that I don't take care of my face.
She buys me creams and lotions to clear my skin
even though she knows I don't play that game.

I hate the way girls *fool* themselves
by using eye liner and mascara, as if
popularity comes in a tube.

She says *one day I'll have to learn to play the game*
like she does every day, preparing for battle,
putting on her armour, layer by layer.

But *I* know I won't because that's
not the kind of life I want:
corporate.

Doloroso ma sognado

Sorrowful but dreamy

Mary

I like the way
minor scales dip
down, like
a landing bird.

Minor scales remind me
of the deep pangs
that strike me
when I see
something sad,
like the kid
who eats alone
in the corner,
tipped away
from the crowd,
his sandwich
cut in four,
in a way that says
someone at home
loves him.

Minor scales suit the space
where I practice—
two hours every day
that go by in a haze
as if the music happens
in other time,
not world time
but music time.

When I play my piano,
images whirl and twirl
in my head, filling
the room with colour.

I'd love to take
those colours
with me to school,
but they hide
without the music.

Sometimes, during the day,
I'll get a spark,
quick and fleeting,
but there's too much
people-noise
for that colour
to break through.

SOMEONE BIG
Mark

My Mini gives me wheels
to go
wherever
I want
whenever
I want.

Nothing holds me back since I bought her
with the insurance money
from my dad's accident,

Second-hand, reconditioned
by a Mini Man:
two black stripes
over the hood,
cosmic wheels
chrome fenders
from the '50s.

My mom says my dad wouldn't have wanted me
to waste the money on a car. He would've wanted me
to use it for school because that was his dream for me,
to become someone big like a brain surgeon
or lawyer or engineer, even though

I was already a grade behind
when he collided head-on with a truck,
driving his cab: two weeks in Intensive Care
draining into sacs, his insides leaking out,
attached to so many tubes he looked like the back
of our TV, hooked to the satellite, DVD, and Xbox.

My Mini surrounds me
like a second skin,
hard and bright.

My dad had no second skin.

The truck crushed his cab so bad,
he and the metal became one. Bits
of it were buried with him, lodged
deep in his limbs and chest.

I picture those pieces shining
in the grave when everything else
has turned to dust.

Getting the Hang of it
Christopher

I'm the guy
who stands too straight,
who can't seem to get the hang
of hanging loose.

My body won't let go,
it wants to be rigid
because so much anxiety
is making it hard
to lighten up
and untighten up
enough to stop
looking
like a jerk
when Annabelle's around.

Just the sight of her
clenches my jaw
hardens my hands
turns me to granite,

even though inside
my thoughts of her
are soft
and tender
and warm.

When she walks by,
I'm a stone statue
standing stiff
as a guard
at Buckingham Palace,

While inside
I'm reaching
beseeching
her to see

Past this rock face
to the funny guy
I know I can be
and would be
if I could learn
the key
to feeling at ease
when Annabelle sees me.

Why Stacey Dumped Us
Annabelle

Because after *ten years* of being best friends
with me and Mary, her ego
exploded

And now she sees herself as much *bigger* than us,
like she is perched on some
high peak,

Queen of the World, while *we*
are just lowly
worms.

All because some guy named Paul liked her
and told her she was hot
and tried

To get into her bikini, the yellow one
she always ties in a double
knot,

Like she's the *first girl in history* who's ever
been seduced at a summer
cottage.

When she came back, she was *bursting* with
superiority, rolling her eyes
at us

Like everything we said was childish and *way
too simple* for her sophisticated
ears.

She tried to describe how it all happened, the kiss
out on the rock and the rest, but stopped
halfway

Because nothing we could picture in our little brains
could match the grandeur of the
real thing.

HOT
Mark

Stacey is short skirts and long legs
in my peripheral vision
when I steer.

She is soft curves when I reach
over into the glove
compartment.

She is loads of laughter in my ear
when the sound of traffic
gets me down.

I never noticed her much before
this year, but now
here she is,

Day after day, riding with me,
stroking my hand
on the shift,

Making my heart race and my feet
push the pedal
even harder.

Talent Show
Annabelle

Talent Show posters line the walls,
auditions coming up.

I want Mary to try out
but she's scared
because Stacey is doing make-up
and the rest of her crowd
everything else, except for
lights and sound, which the AV Club
is eager to do.

Mary will have to place her ego
in their hands and trust
it doesn't get crushed,
like a bird.

Besides, says Mary,
Chopin's a nerd
to that crowd.
They'll want rock bands
or pop stars
with bellies showing
or hip-hop dancers
in army fatigues.

Mary plays so well it's scary.
Her hands dance
across the keys

And I always wonder what she sees:
    a forest of silver trees
    or a frosted moonscape
    of sparkling craters,
    the perfect place
    for her music to soar
    above the galaxy?

Con Forza
With force
Mary

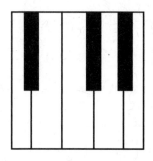

My piano teacher is pushing me
to audition for the Talent Show.

It's like a conspiracy,
everyone wanting me to play.

He says:
It's a shame not to share
your music with the world.
It's like a painter
never showing her art
or a poet never reading her words.

My mom says:
Why did we pay for all those lessons
if you won't play in public?

My dad says:
Listen to your mom!

I say:
When I'm not playing
parts of me drift, like notes
lifted off the bars, floating
aimlessly in space.

Isn't it enough that I feel best
when I'm playing, that playing
makes me feel most like the me
I was meant to be?

Isn't that worth your money, Mother,
or would you rather see me
in pieces, lost, with nothing
to make me whole?

Lucky
Stacey

I know I'm not Mark's first girlfriend,
but I think he likes me best.

The rest were all too clingy, always wanting
him to call and take them to the mall.

They didn't understand that Mark
needs to keep moving
and only he can decide
where he wants to go.

Sure, he wants you beside him
but you've got to be willing
to bend in and buckle up
and put up with his moods,
ride them out with him,
no matter where they lead.

Sometimes, we drive all the way
to the border, where
he'll park and stare
as though he's plotting
his escape.

At moments like that
you have to sit still, keep
your mouth shut and wait
until he's worked it out.

Then he comes back
and sees you
and remembers
how lucky he is
to have you there,
all pretty and sexy
in your tightest clothes.
You can feel him shift
toward you, his eyes
glossy, his pants straining.

You've waited hours for that look
because it makes you feel
a thousand feet tall,
even though he still hasn't
said a single word.

Just Because

Christopher

My friends tell me
to forget it.

Girls like her
don't go out
with guys
like me.

They say it
like I have
a disease,

Just because
I'm shy
like them

And good at school
and belong to
the AV Club
like them

And have acne
like some
of them.

None of those things
mean I don't
have feelings.

Even Galileo
knew that all things
fall at the same rate

Whether they're
light as
feathers

Or heavy
as stone,
like me.

Social Action Group
Annabelle

I've been seeing signs for their meetings
since school started: kids
at sewing machines, kids
outside tin shacks, kids
weaving carpets, kids
bent over in fields; underneath,
the words *Do you care?*

Yesterday, I *finally* found the nerve
to go to the meeting
in the small room
with no windows
behind the boiler
in the basement.

Mr. Dawe wears cargo pants
with a hundred pockets,
sandals, and t-shirts
with slogans like *Ban the bomb*
and *Make love, not war*, and
his gray hair is a skinny ponytail
down his back.

When I walk in, he says
Welcome, comrade,
and the five kids sitting
in a circle on the floor
laugh and say hello
and I have never felt
so *welcome* in my life.

Mr. Dawe talks with his hands,
waving them around
like he is conducting
an orchestra; we are
the musicians, rehearsing
a score, making plans
for a booth on child labour
and the war in Iraq.

Why not plant two flowers
with one seed? Mr. Dawe asks
and I think how, if my mom
had said that, she'd have used
the one about killing birds
with a single stone.

THESE KIDS
Mr. Dawe

These kids turn me on—Hey,
get your minds out of the gutter!

I mean in an intellectual way:
the way they think, the things they care about.

It's not all Hollywood superstars
and fashion and fast cars.

Well, at least not for these committed kids
who come to the weekly meetings in that crap room.

If the school really cared about education, as in
the Latin *educere*, to lead, they'd put their money

Where their proverbial mouths are and give us some cash
for a better space and a computer.

They just don't get that these kids might be
the Kings, the Ghandis, the Mandelas, the Suu Kyis

Of their generation; it has been a complete
privilege for me to work alongside them.

I'd rather be with them and their energy and spirit
than sit through protocol and curriculum meetings

With my colleagues. Some of them are more burnt
out than lava and haven't had a new thought

In their heads since they rolled off the assembly line
at college, diplomas in their fists, forty years ago.

It's like there's some fascist policy up there that says
IF IT TURNS KIDS ON, IT'S GOT TO BE BAD FOR THEM.

When John Lennon said, *Whatever gets you through the night*
he meant *night* as a metaphor for any hard place, like school.

I know that. These kids know it. Why not get through
AND change the world in the process?

MY STEEL SHELL
Mark

When I drive to school
I always hope
people are standing around
because no one can help
looking at my yellow Mini.

It's bright as the sun,
speedy and slick.

I weave it in and out
of those concrete pillars
meant to slow cars down
on school property.

We're supposed to brake,
but I just twist around them
smooth as a snake.

Sometimes people clap,
but not the principal.

When she sees me
she calls me in
and gives me
a lecture
on safety
on being responsible
on how a car isn't a toy
but a machine that has the power
to kill, as if I don't know that.
She sounds like my mother
warning me about speed:

Haven't I lost enough already?
Mom always says.
Don't they know that when I'm in
my yellow Mini I'm safe,
impervious?

The car is my thick skin
and when I'm
in it nothing,
nothing,
can sink
in.

My Dad
Annabelle

I can't help wondering what he
was like, or *is* like, because he's not *dead*,
he's just not *here*, in my life.

My mom tells me I don't need
to know him, that knowing him
wouldn't *change* who I am.

But how does she *know* that? It's like
the one about the tree falling in the forest
when no one is there to hear it. Doesn't it still fall?

I guess I'm kind of like the tree, only
my father isn't around to see me.
Maybe I'd grow *differently* if he were.

My mom grew up near here, so I might
have passed my dad a million times,
maybe even handed him a flyer at the mall.

If I did, I wonder what he did with it: did he read it,
or ditch it? Is he the type of guy who *cares* about things
like child labour? Does the world keep him up at night

Or is he the type of guy who only cares about hockey
and football, watching TV with a beer in one hand,
a cigarette in the other, swearing at the screen?

Either way, I'd like to *know* because it might help me
figure myself out, it might help me see what kind
of life I'll have when I'm older, not that I expect

To become *exactly* like my mom or dad, but
it would be nice to know that I inherited *some* traits,
instead of feeling everything about me starts at zero.

Ostinato

Persistent

Mary

I hear her, tip-toeing
down the stairs,
crouching

In the stairwell, like
an intruder,
trying

To figure out what's keeping me
down here for
hours.

It's like she thinks I can't
hear her
breathing

Or scratching her hair, or tapping
her fingers on
her knees

Like she's a human metronome
decoding my music
in the dark.

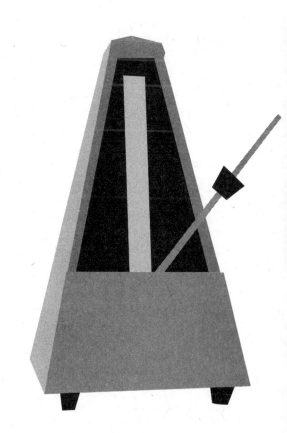

Things She Doesn't Want to Know

Annabelle

My mom says:
> Why don't you hang out
> with Stacey anymore?
> You used to be over there all the time
> and now, nothing. Has something happened
> that you're not telling me about?

She thinks I put Stacey off by telling her
things she doesn't *want* to know
about the clothes she wears.

As if I would.
I don't even *speak* to Stacey anymore,
but I can't help it if she reads our posters.

It's the type of info my mother thinks
I should keep to myself because
it won't win me any friends.

My mom says Mr. Dawe is a leftover hippie.
She can tell by the fluff between his toes
that he shows off in Birkenstocks, and
by his shirts that never smell clean
but are rumpled and musty.

She says he shouldn't encourage us to protest
like that in public, that it might *harm*
our image, *prevent* us from
getting summer jobs.
I say some things are more *important*
than money.

The school agrees with my mom
and they've told Mr. Dawe not to
take us off school property,
as if we *belong* to the school, like
the gym mats or desks.

Don't they know we have
our own free will?

Sure, Mr. Dawe led us there, but *now*
we are ready to go ahead,
even without him.

Poem

Christopher

I need to send her
a sign to tell
her

How I feel because
until I do
I am

Just some guy she walks by,
blended in,
instead

Of a guy who is bursting
with feeling
for her.

I need to put myself
in her sphere, her
orbit

Like one of
Jupiter's
small moons.

I could write a poem
comparing her to a
flower,

The perfect rosy petals
of her cheeks
blushing,

The delicate stems of her
fingers waving when
she talks

About things she really
cares about,
fiery

As a rose in full bloom,
each velvet petal
folding

One on top of the other
the way I'd like
to fold

Annabelle
in my
arms.

This New Guy
Annabelle

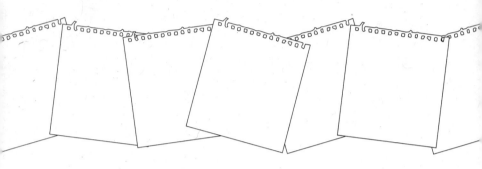

On Saturday, this new guy
shows up and he doesn't know
how to *persist* when people
reject the flyer.

I tell him:
You have to
stick it under an arm
or on top of a bag.

You have to
act like it's the most
important paper ever printed.

You have to
push when pushing
is against your nature.

You have to
smile even when someone
is cursing you.

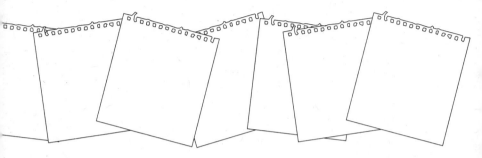

You have to
stay hopeful even when you see
your flyers crushed

Under the wheels
of a thousand
cars,

Which is not
always easy
to do.

Trying to Change the World
Christopher

I can't get the hang
of standing
and handing
out the flyers.

I feel I am
being rude
when I say:
Do you know this store
buys from suppliers
who use sweatshops?

I can't stand
seeing people's eyes
hit the ground,
or the way they
tuck in their chins
and skulk through
the doors,
some grasping
the flyers, others
waving them away
like wasps.

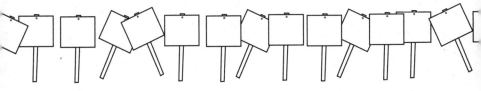

I try to study
Annabelle
to see how she
does it, her technique
as smooth as honey,
always pleasant,
like she is handing
out candy
and not bad news.

Once or twice she smiles
at me, nods
to encourage me,
and it makes the day
worthwhile,
makes me glad
to be standing
in the October cold
trying to change
the world.

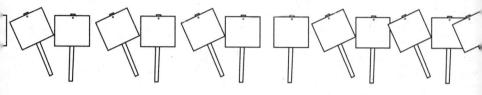

Watching her flick
her hair
out of her eyes
and blow the tips
of her fingers
to keep warm
makes me want
to wrap
myself around her
like the fuzzy blanket
my mom bought
at this store
last week.

At the end of the day,
frozen, we all stop off
for hot chocolate.

When Annabelle
blows a hole into
the whipped cream,
a dab of it clings
to her upper lip.

I want
to lick it off.

The Truth

Annabelle

My mom says people don't always *want*
to know the truth.

She says if *everyone* knew the truth
about *everything*

In the world, no one would *ever*
get out of bed.

But what if knowing just a *piece*
of the truth

Changes *one little thing* that a person
does or thinks?

Like the challenge Mr. Dawe
just gave me

For our Hallowe'en info-booth
in the lobby.

This is *one piece* I've discovered
so far:

Factories in Bangladesh
are full of kids whose fingers
bleed. They sleep
on planks in dorms,
their stomachs rumbling.
Their schooling has ended,
the whole balloon
of their childhood pierced
and emptied in a flash
by a sewing machine needle
so that people like Stacey
can buy skinny jeans
that cling to their bony hips.

Glad He Didn't See It

Mark's Mom

Your father would be rolling
    over in his grave
    if he could see the way
    you are turning out,
        hanging out with kids
        who are allowed to stay
        out all night long
        and never open a book.

Your last report card
    a long row of D's and F's
    with comments like
        lacks motivation
        not trying
        shows disrespect.

It almost made me glad your father
    didn't have to see it. His
    face would have fallen,
    the lines around his mouth
    grown tighter and deeper.
        All those years of driving
        a cab to the airport,
        fighting traffic,
        hauling bags,
        so you could get
        the education he missed
        out on back in Lebanon
        because his family
        had to flee the war
        when he was fifteen.

And now this yellow car,
       your constant companion,
     a new girl every month
          her head hanging out the window
          like a gargoyle,
          flashing a pretty smile
          at the world.

What does her mother think?
     Does she know her daughter
     is out till all hours
          driving around
          god knows where
          doing god knows what?

And, if she does, is she
     as scared as me?

OMEN
Mark
_____

My dad thought he would always have
           good luck.

That's because, when he was a kid,
           a bomb

Landed on the roof of his apartment
           building

But didn't explode. It simply sat there,
           ticking.

His friend, who climbed up, said it looked like a
           creature,

A black bird of death that sent everyone
           scrambling

Into the streets and throwing stuff down from
           windows.

My dad didn't see it as death, but as an
           omen

That he was somehow protected,
           special.

I think it just took death a long time to
           find him.

Ordinary
Annabelle

I don't want to be *ordinary*.

You see ordinary people everywhere:
at the grocery store, loading their carts,
looking tired, checking the prices,
shuffling along like zombies.

Or where my mom and I have breakfast
every Sunday. We always get the waitress
with frizzy hair and she always asks the same thing,
Sunny-side-up or over-easy.

I wonder what her life is like:
       does she have talents
       she didn't nurture
       or did she always dream
       of waiting on tables
       at the Greek deli
       where bloated pickles
       float in humongous jars?

When I ask my mom
she tells me not to be a snob,
then she shakes her head at me
like she can't figure out why
I wonder about such *stupid* things.

I think she forgets what it's like
to worry about your future
and ponder what kind of life
you might have one day
when you have no talent
and when you're an *idiot,*
because you can't walk past
a lounge just because
your ex-best friend is there
on the other side, inside
a group you were both in awe of
just last year.

Mr. Dawe says I have a talent
for organizing people
and motivating them
to take action.

But can I make a *future* out of that?

Agitato

Agitated, with excitement

Mary

In my basement, I like to shine
the reading lamp down
on my piano, but keep the rest
of the room dark.

That way I can pretend I'm
anywhere—La Scala,
Carnegie Hall, Covent Garden,
the great music halls of the world.

But in this auditorium
the bright lights trap me
at the out-of-tune piano.

My mom bribed me
with a trip to New York
to see Angela Hewitt,
who has magical hands.

They had to roll the piano out
from behind a mountain of props
on three squeaky wheels, the
dust sheet trailing behind like a veil.

I'm on right after some dancers,
so the smell of sweat and powder
lingers on stage, along with the *thump*
thump thump of their music, dark
like bats caught in the rafters.

My hands hover like hummingbirds
over the keys, my eyes
on the string of black dots,
my foot a brick, poised
above the pedals.

Slowly, I enter the music,
blocking out the stage and its
dusty shadows, where the judges' faces
are tipped toward me

Until my music is all there is,
floating, cascading,
circling back into itself,
loopy as a butterfly,
red and gold.

Even the third-floor crowd
is hushed, pulled in,
just like my teacher said
they would be.

No one, he said, *can resist
the lure of Chopin,
not even the kids
of your generation.*

Could he be right?

Love Poem

Christopher

I wrote her a poem
and slipped it in
her pocket
at the meeting
to plan
the next
protest.

I wasn't sure if I'd
go back, but how
else can I get close
to Annabelle?

I hope she finds it
(or not, both
options are scary)
because it took me
hours and hours
to compose.

You make me feel
tall in a small world
loud in the silence
bright in the dark
simply by your presence
which is warm rain
on my parched soul

But I didn't
have the nerve
to sign it.

There's no way
she'll think
of me first.

She'll scan
our faces
at the mall,
seeking
clues.

If I send her
the right one,
a wink
a nod
a smile,
she'll know.

But then I might
have to watch
her face fall

in dis
            appoint
                    ment.

It's a Good Thing
Stacey

If my parents knew how late
I stayed out last night,
they'd flip.

When we crossed
the bridge back into town
the sun was already rising,
lighting up the tops
of tall buildings
like candles.

Earlier, Mark parked
by a lake and we watched
the water grow dark
as the sun set.

It grew so black
I couldn't tell
where land ended
and water
began.

Mark didn't budge,
didn't say a word
for hours, just kept
staring straight
ahead, like he was
waiting for something
to emerge from the lake.

I knew to just sit silently
beside him because
when Mark gets quiet
it turns all sound
into noise, like
everything around
him has to shut
off, including
me.

It's a good thing
I know that because
that's what Mark likes
about me, the fact that
I know what to do—
how to be pretty
and wait until he's ready
to notice me.

If my parents knew
how late we came home
they'd kill me.

It's a good thing
they sleep
so deeply
and fall for
the jumble
of blankets
I lay out
to make it seem
like I'm at home,
sleeping
deeply
too.

Stacey's Sister's Diary
Annabelle

I was at Stacey's when her sister
        came home and announced
        she was engaged to this guy
        her parents *hadn't even met.*

Her mom put down the pot
        she was scrubbing
        and dried her hands
        on the dish towel slowly.

Her dad put down his paper,
        (I think it was the first time
        I ever saw his whole face)
        and leaned forward in his chair.

The kitchen was completely silent,
        except for the hum of the fridge
        and the drip of the tap
        and five noses breathing.

Stacey kicked me gently
        under the table
        and I kicked back
        because we both *knew*

What her sister, only eighteen,
        had been up to: she laid
        it all out *in graphic detail*
        in the diary we could open with a pin.

We knew her sister had been *doing it*
    for months in John's father's car,
    parked behind some warehouses,
    her left foot braced on the gear shift.

They'd done it on the hill behind the arena,
    her back jabbing against
    some rocks, John's socks
    vanishing in the stream beside them.

And they'd found an abandoned mattress
    in a lane downtown and fooled around
    like a couple of alley cats, scratching
    their skin on loose coils.

We read the pages over and over,
    curled up under the covers,
    our flashlight burning the paper,
    giggling and gagging.

And now they were going to get married
    and turn into a *respectable couple*
    who'd shop for end tables
    and a matching double bed.

That's it for the diaries, Stacey said.
    In nine months I'll be an aunt,
    my sister will be fat,
    and I'll have to try to look at John

Without turning beet red
    because in my head
    I'll be seeing them at it
    in all those weird places.

But Stacey's sister didn't marry John
    or have a baby. She moved out
    west instead, with another guy,
    taking her diary with her.

I wonder if Stacey's doing those things
    now with Mark, parked
    on some dead end street,
    scrunched up inside the Mini.

Does she think of her sister's words
    and try to copy her moves,
    or is she so *in love*
    her mind is blank?

And does she ever think of me
    reading those pages with her,
    burying our screams
    in her pillows?

HIS LAST THOUGHT OF ME
Mark

Driving out, getting away,
ribbons of highway
beneath my wheels,
is the only way I feel
real these days.

It's like my Mini and I have morphed,
like those transformer toys
I used to play with,
twisting joints
to turn hulky heroes
into mean machines.

My dad used to say he wished
he could fold up his cab
that way and become a big
strong man, with blades
for fingers, exhaust blasting
out of his heels, speeding
him away from the concrete
he spent his life driving on.

He always talked about Lebanon,
its white Mediterranean beaches,
twisty cedars and ancient ruins,
as if nothing here could compete,
not even me.

He was always comparing
me to my cousins in Beirut,
top of their classes
buckling down, busy
as beavers, building
futures, not

Out having fun
going to parties
dating girls
playing games
making money
flipping burgers.

Sometimes I wonder
if his last thought
was of me, yelling
at him to leave me
the fuck alone.

You Don't Know

Stacey's Mom

Of course I hear you coming in
at all hours, even after
the sun has already
risen.

I can hear the front door click
shut, no matter how softly
you close it. The click is like
a crack of thunder in my brain

And those creaks on the stairs,
as you tiptoe up, are like
deep cracks opening in a quake.

One day, Stacey, the earth will open up
beneath you and swallow you whole,

But what would I have to do
to stop you?

Lock you in your room, tie
you up, kick you out
so that the world will swallow you
even sooner?

Your father's heart is still broken
from your sister's succession of guys
who lured her so far away.

He pretends he doesn't hear you
come in—that way he doesn't have to
deal with you, so I go along, asking
if you had a good sleep when I know
it was only two hours long, or if you're not
feeling well when I know your eyes
are dark and puffy from lack of rest.

It's the car that scares me most.
I've seen the way your boyfriend drives,
zipping in and out like the rules of the road
don't apply to him.

When I watch you leave I think how it's my daughter
he is hauling, my own flesh and blood,
who kept me up countless nights
watching her fight her fevers,
feeding her medicine, chicken soup, and hugs,
for what?

To watch her throw
her life away?

Sotto Voce

In an undertone

Mary

The list is out
and I am in.

Now there's no
turning back:

Rehearsals Tuesdays and Thursdays
3:30 - 6:00 sharp.

I'll be there, but
maybe not sharp.

Sharp is for extroverts
and stage lovers.

Sharp is for people who can
crack up in public

Or talk to strangers
full volume, brazen,

Not sotto voce,
like me.

Make-up
Stacey

I always knew I'd do it one day.

It's something I'm good at, maybe
because of all the time I spent
letting my older sister make me up.

She'd practice on me, like I was
one of those giant-sized doll heads
that come with mini lipsticks and shadow.

She'd make me look ten years older
or, on dark days, like I'd been punched
around the eyes, the lids so blue.

I'm already thinking about what I'll do
for different people, how I'll make
their faces look like they're lit up

From the inside, like I'm a magician
who can flick a switch inside a dull person's
skull, turning them bright.

Mary will be my biggest challenge
with her plain pudgy face and tiny eyes
and lips that are thin as toothpicks.

Too bad I can't ask my sister for advice.

In My Pocket
Annabelle

Standing in the parking lot,
waiting for the others to show,
stamping my feet to keep warm,

I peek into a parked car
and see a couple twisting
toward each other.

Suddenly, his face is on top of hers
and he is eating her lips, not stopping
for air, as if they're kissing
for the *last time* ever.

I touch the note in my coat pocket,
its corners soft from my fingers
bending, creasing and smoothing
down the paper while I try to figure out
who popped it in there.

I can see the others coming,
placards balanced
on their shoulders,
but all I can wonder
is who actually feels
that way about me
and how can I just be
myself, knowing
somebody does?

I admire her drive, the way she finds
the pictures, makes the posters,
assembles the group.

At her age, I was out at parties
or sneaking into bars
with fake IDs.

Youth is so fleeting,
it goes by in a
wink.

It seems like only yesterday
that I was sewing
my grad dress:

Braided straps and pleated skirt—
far too complex for
a novice—

So that, last minute, I was ripping out
the stitches, starting over,
crying, dreading

The fact that the fabric would pull
and pucker around my
middle.

Touch me
Stacey

I watch our town grow smaller
in the side mirror, measuring the buildings
between my thumb and index finger,
pretending to squish them like a bug.

I love leaving my whole world behind
as Mark and I speed along
the highway, music blaring,
my feet on the dash, getting dirty
looks from people
in other cars, giving them
the finger, Mark's gorgeous
dark eyes piercing the road ahead.

We are driving around the mountains,
down winding country roads, some
so steep we crawl, others
only gravel roads for loggers,
not a house in sight, the sun
going down fast and dusk
making monsters of the trees.

At the end of one, he stops and gets out,
leaving me to watch him weave
between trunks, lit by nothing but
the half moon.

I sit here, listening to
owls hooting,
branches cracking,
November wind
rustling dead leaves,

my eyes straining
to see between
the black branches,
the car growing colder
by the minute.
I wonder if there are
bears in these mountains,
and what if Mark doesn't
come back and I can't
drive because he's taken the keys
and my cell phone signal is dead?

Would my parents come look for me?
They didn't look for my sister when she left.
Sure, they knew where she'd gone
and even had her new address,
but shouldn't they have looked for her
anyway?

Then suddenly Mark appears,
the moon catching the zipper
of his jacket, turning him into
a vertical streak of silver.

At school he's all over me:
hands, arms, legs always
wrapping round me, but
now, when we're parked
out of town, he
doesn't try
to touch me.

He just fires up the Mini
and zigzags us back
to civilization.

FOUND IT
Mark

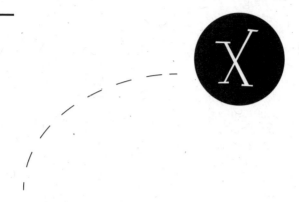

I think I found it, the piece
of land my dad dreamed of buying,
surrounded by pine trees that grew high enough
to touch the clouds.

It's pretty dark here in the woods,
looking for the stream, listening
for the trickling sound
that pulled me in as a kid.

My dad found it first shot—no bad turns
for him when it came to navigating roads—
he'd have found it blind-folded because
he had an internal compass and always

Knew where to steer, except that one icy day
when no amount of swerving worked,
the force of nature pulling the truck toward him
like two tons of death.

Pinch Pinch

Christopher

I keep doing it because I can't
believe it's real.

Annabelle didn't cringe
when I confessed.

She turned redder than me,
rosy apple red,

And when I took her hand
there was a spark.

Her eyes widened as it dawned
on her that it was me,

Then she pulled out the poem,
crumpled and creased,

And I nodded and said,
I hope you liked it,

And I could tell by her smile
that she did.

Then the door banged open
and the others clomped in,

Shattering our moment
like glass.

How do You Know
Annabelle

When someone is it?

It's not like a game of tag
     where you count,
     eyes-closed,
     against a tree
     then run squealing
     and tag the slowest
     runner.

Christopher wasn't even *running*.

He was *standing* right next to me
     like he was a tree
     that I could've leaned
     against and he would've
     wrapped his arms
     like branches around me.

I'd never really *looked* at him too closely before.

But now, only inches away,
     his big brown eyes drinking me in,
     his hand brushing back my hair,
     his tall body bending toward me
     as if he wanted to blend into me,
     I *saw* him for the first time.

And now I'm wondering: what will next time be like?

Will it be hard to stand around handing out flyers,
    trying to get people to see what's wrong
    with the world when Christopher is around,
    because all I'll want to do is stand near him
    and see if he looks at me like that again,
    because when he did, something in me flipped,
    making an acrobat of my emotions?

SAILING
Mark
_____

The lake was in the middle
 of the woods, ringed by maples
  with buckets set in to trap
   the sap trickling in spring.

My dad made boats out of newspaper,
 folded over and over and over in a way
  I could never follow and then coated
   with shoe spray to keep them afloat.

We raced to see whose boat
 could float the farthest, like
  a mini regatta in the woods, our
   leaf flags flapping in the breeze.

He said the boats would sail
 all summer long, bumping
  into canoes and strange fish
   long after we'd disappeared,

And he'd enjoy seeing them in his head
 as he zoomed down the gray highway
  to the airport, surrounded by nothing
   but concrete and cars and smog.

It made me mad that the boats
 didn't come back, but he said
  it was always good to leave your mark:
   I suppose I am his.

How Could She?

Stacey

I saw her with Christopher.
He's always been such a loser.
I can't believe she'd go out with him.

It's like she's lost her senses and can't see
his pimply skin or geeky neck that sticks
out of those shirts his mom buys for him.

It makes me wonder how we used to be friends
and what we ever had in common, which
couldn't have been much because I could never

Go near someone like Christopher who's so
different from Mark, who's so gorgeous
and built, hot enough to be a model.

When I saw them, they were holding hands
and he hung onto every word she said as they
walked past our lounge, oblivious to everything.

I called to her but she didn't even blink. It was like
they were walking on the moon, they were so into
each other, Christopher smiling and nodding

While she was talking,
their shoulders tapping like glasses
as if every word was a celebration.

Crescendo

Increasing gradually in volume

Mary

Today's the first rehearsal
and I'm already
regretting trying out.

Stacey is working
make-up.

I bet she can't wait
to get her hands on me,
to make me over
into a monster, just
to amuse herself.

Will it look rude if I
bring a book and simply
nestle in a chair, incognito,
until it's my turn on stage
or will they expect me
to be part of the whole

Rah rah rah thing, the entire cast and crew spinning
a web of excitement, rising in crescendo until
the big night when the bright lights go on
and the backstage sizzle carries us
out there to dazzle the crowd?

Will anyone mind
if I just watch
from afar?

What Stacey Thinks
Annabelle

I wonder what Stacey thinks
when she sees me with Christopher.

Does she remember the way kids mocked him
because he stuttered like a machine gun?

Does she wonder how I can touch him
when his skin has patches of acne?

Does she compare him to Paul and Mark
and beam at how well they fare?

Do I care?
At first I did.

I was shy to hold his hand at school, knowing
everyone would look and point and talk.

But we hung on tight and now no one cares,
except Stacey, who always glares

When we walk into the auditorium
and climb the stairs to the glass booth

Where Christopher and his friends
are working the sound and lights.

Christopher showed me how to throw the big switch
And flood the stage with light, exposing

Every square inch, even the dusty corners.
It reminded me of the way Stacey stares,

Illuminating every part of me, taking me in, frame
by frame, like she's storing away the image.

It makes me uneasy because I don't know *what
she's planning to do with it.*

I Never did Know Mary
Stacey

Even though we were a constant
threesome

Annabelle was always our
go between,

As if Mary could only be
reflected

To me through the mirror of
Annabelle,

So that now, when I watch her
play Chopin,

It's like watching someone I've
never met,

Someone mysterious, with
hidden depths.

I'd never have expected
such music

To flow from her fingers
so freely,

Because she always struck me
as heavy,

All locked up inside her
closed-off self.

Even the way she walks—head
pointing down,

Blocking out the world around her,
blinkers on,

Oblivious to everything
important,

Like who's walking by, or who to
look good for,

Who to laugh for, who to shine for,
who to perform for,

In the hallways of high school as
expected.

When I do her makeup I'm
supposed to

Accentuate her features and
make them pop,

But I think I'll use white powder to
efface her

And dress her in white to
erase her

So all that's left is sound:
sensual.

A word I never would have used
for Mary.

Overture
Mary's Mom

She's doing it and that's all that
matters.

It has to be a step in the right
direction.

I hope it will be the start of
something,

Take her outside the tight
little world

She's built in the basement,
playing

Piano in the near dark, her music
spreading

Along the floorboards, like a
colony

Of musical mice who stop
scurrying

The minute anyone else
appears.

Christopher Is

Annabelle

Christopher is the guy *no* one
notices,
standing behind his locker door
to hide his
tall and lanky body and his
pimply face.

Christopher is the guy who gets
the *best* grades
and turns beet red delivering
French orals
but can whiz through an algebra
equation
on the board at the speed of light
times twenty.

Christopher is the guy who's been
in my class
since grade *one*, front row and centre
quiet, shy,
kicking soccer balls in the yard
at recess,
never showing off or seeking
attention.

Christopher is the guy who held
my hand so
tenderly and looked into my eyes
so deeply
that he turned into someone *new*
and handsome,
the chocolate brown of his eyes
suddenly
delicious.

NEVER LONG ENOUGH
Mark

The road is never long enough.

I've got to find a way to go farther.

One day I'll keep going and never look back,

Leave school and Stacey and my house and mother behind,

Especially my mother because I can't stand the way she now
has to speak for my father

So that even though he's gone his words are still a constant
chatter of disappointment in my ears

Until I feel I'll scream and never stop screaming so loud
my relatives will hear me all the way across the continents
in Lebanon

And maybe hop on a plane and come over to check out what's
happening to the only part of the family that moved away to
the new world, the land of opportunity,

Only to find a two-bedroom apartment in an old run-down
complex with rusty balconies where my mother spends all her time
crying and wondering why my father had to die

Except they won't find me because I'll have found the nerve to just
keep driving, all the way west or south, even though the police
will stop me wherever I go because I'm a young guy with
olive-skin and an Arabic last name.

Injustice

Annabelle

It's what I see
        when people's carts are loaded
        with stuff: stuffed bears,
        cartoon slippers
        and plastic Santas.

What *I* see is
        stuff *nobody* really needs:
        tacky, cheap, made
        by people who have
        nothing.

What *my mom* sees is
        harmless stuff
        bought with love
        for family fun.

She *doesn't* see is
        tin shacks with no floors
        sick kids with no medicine
        bucket toilets and dirty water
        empty plates and bloated bellies.

She says I shouldn't
        think so much about things
        that happen *so far away*
        in places where people
        are grateful for any job.

She blames Mr. Dawe
        for filling our heads
        with negative thoughts
        and making us see the world
        as one big ugly place.

But *I* say
        not seeing the world
        that way is what
        made the world
        that way in the first place .

Christopher says
        we're both right
        but that's *not*
        what I wanted
        to hear.

Now
Christopher

Now, we're the dynamic
duo, standing
near the doors,
enlightening
the zombies
shopping
blindly,
unaware,
like I was
before
Annabelle.

Now, we're a force
that can't be
ignored,
the two of us
so close,
two flyers
coming at them,
two bodies
to sidestep
or stare
down.

Now, when our fingers
freeze, we reach
for each others'
and feel the heat
flow back in
through
our gloves.

Now, if only I could forget
what we're really
doing here.

RULES OF THE ROAD
Christopher's Father

Suddenly you are
taller
smarter
deeper
older
and slightly colder
to me,

Like you think
if you get too close
you will become
a child again.

I'd like to give you
advice,
tell you that
how you act now will
shape the man
you become,
set the stage
for future
relationships,
form the prototype
against which
you measure
your success,

But I'm no longer
at the helm,
steering
the toboggan
with you clinging
to my back,
or leading the way
through traffic
on our bikes,
teaching you
the rules of the road,
your hand
seeking mine
at street corners,
waiting for lights
to turn green.

The only thing
in front of you
now is your conscience.

May it steer you
well.

On the Inside

Annabelle

Mr. Dawe encourages us
to enter the mall
instead of standing
like stone pillars
at the doors, as though
we have *no right*
to be inside, among
the shoppers.

He says we'd have more
impact getting them
right at the scene
of their crimes, our
actions doubled
in glass storefronts,
the innocent shoppers
caught by our lures:

Powder blue flyers
designed to resemble
promo-junk, two-for-one,
buy-one-get-one-free,
except that when they
open them they see
Asian girls sleeping
in a toy factory dorm
tight as a submarine,

Two rows of bunks
stretching forever,
like an image caught
in a dressing room
mirror, reflecting
into infinity, which
is what their days
must feel like, seven
to ten, short breaks
and little food.

I wonder if they sometimes
stab their fingers on
their needles just to jab
themselves awake and
if they do, do they
think of Sleeping Beauty,
who at least got to sleep
for one hundred years
before being rescued
by Prince Charming?

Modulation
A harmonic progression

Mary

It does get easier,
just like my teacher said
it would, playing
in front of a crowd.

I remind myself that
even Chopin said
the days leading up to
a performance were hell.

I like knowing that Annabelle
and Christopher are up there
controlling the lights.

I can feel them sending
warm vibes over
the third floor crowd
whose reactions I can never read.

The first few weeks my stomach
roiled like a stormy sea, my fingers
slipped on the keys, and my feet
clomped across the stage.

Once, the bench scraped back
by mistake, echoing
like a long fart
through the air.

Another time I turned my page
too hard and sent the sheets
fluttering, out of order,
to the floor.

But most days nothing bad happens and
I simply play, forgetting about people,
focusing only on the music
that flows from my fingers

Letting it spin a colourful cocoon around me,
hiding me until the director
shouts "next" and I
can leave.

Pearl
Annabelle

Mary is like a pearl when
she plays, so shiny
and polished.

Before, she was *inside* the oyster
and no one knew she
could play

Except me and her parents
and her teacher.
I hope

That when Christopher does the lights,
he turns them on her
full blast

To make sure she stands out
because knowing Mary
as I do

She will want to crawl inside
the shell of the
piano

And curl up there,
tiny as a grain
of sand.

Inside the Mall
Christopher

I was okay with parking lots
and sidewalks, and sticking flyers
under windshield wipers,
and marching in a circle
round and round
outside the entrance.

But going inside was another story,
especially when my aunt
stepped out of The Gap
with my cousin's present
looped over her arm.

She started to walk toward me
but I turned away and froze,
hoping she'd get the message
and stay away. Then

I had to watch Annabelle
run up to her and shove
a flyer inside the blue bag.

I wondered: would my aunt
wrap it up with the present?

Opening Me Up
Annabelle

Christopher
  opens me up
  like a room
  I never knew I had.

Inside
  that room is a *me*
  who laughs
  and kisses his neck
  and combs his hair
  with my fingers.

Last night
  walking from
  his house to mine,
  after rehearsal,
  counting our steps
  but losing track
  after two thousand,
  the numbers trailing
  away in giggles
  that turned to kisses

Christopher
     said, *let's kiss*
     every prime number
     so we did: 1, 3, 5, 7, 11, 13, 17, 19, 23, 29, 31, 37
     until the kisses grew
     too far between.
     Let's kiss every
     even number, I said
     so we did, kissing
     every second step
     until we were at my door,
     the light in my mom's
     room telling me she
     was up, waiting.

Hiding
     behind a bush
     Christopher asked
     if I knew how far
     we were from
     Venus, and when I
     shook my head he said,
     40,400,000 kilometers
     which is how far I feel
     from you when you're here
     and I'm at home.

We kissed
        behind the bush, away
        from the light until
        we heard the front
        door open and saw
        my mom sniff
        the night air, as if
        she could smell
        our wanting
        each other
        so bad.

Christopher
        said *480 degrees—*
        that's the temperature
        of two things:
        Venus and me
        right now

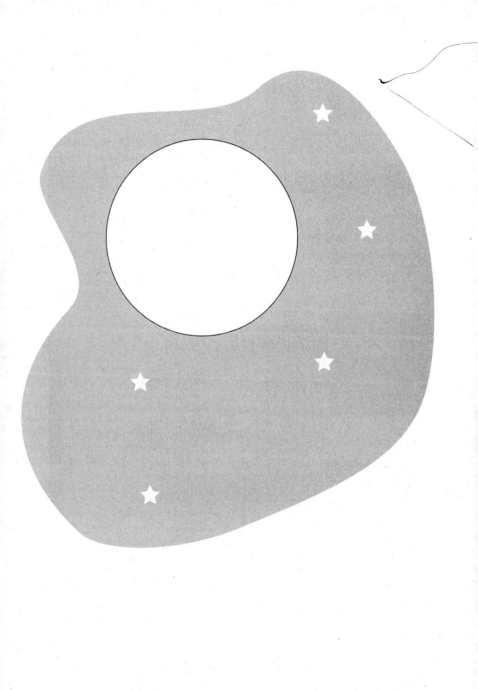

I Know How It Happens

Annabelle's Mom

That first kiss, that first real kiss
where you feel yourself
go hot all
over

And the whole world melts away
until there is just the two
of you in a vacuum
of sound and
touch

That is when it happens, the heat
rising, your bodies groping
more and more toward
each other, leaving
your rational
mind be-
hind.

That's how it happened for me at
sixteen at a party, upstairs,
the thump of the music
below, like our
pulses turned
on high

And next thing I knew I'd done it,
clothes half on, half off, in a
stranger's bed with a guy
I barely knew, his beer
breath asking if I was
okay and me acting
tough, saying yes,
when really I
was wet and
scared.

Nine months later Annabelle arrived,
pink and precious, named after my
favourite Poe poem, one line
now so true: *I was a child*
and she was a child,
the two of us raw
and kicking,
fighting
for life.

So I know how it happens, Annabelle.

Against Me
Annabelle

Today, the waitress at the deli
put my plate down and smiled
right at me, as if she could see
into my heart—*big and bursting*
like the red pepper in the jar.

I made a happy face of my meal,
two eggs sunny side up
a tomato nose and bacon mouth,
and my mom asked what's gotten
into me, *as if she doesn't know.*

When she met Christopher, she shook
his hand hard, squeezing it
like she wanted to *trap* it
and make sure he couldn't
use it against me.

WEIGHT

Mark

Her presence is starting to weigh me down.

She wants something from me, something
I thought I wanted to give her,
but can't.

My dad used to weigh me down, too.

His expectations sat on my shoulders,
dark and heavy as that bomb
on his roof.

My mom does it to me too, at home.

The way she shuffles around, sighing heavily, like
she's looking for signs to tell her
which way to go.

Alien
Christopher

My friends treat me like aliens have
beamed me up and snuck
an android into
my body.

It's like they can't figure out how
I got Annabelle to go out
with me, a former
nobody.

They don't know whether they can slap
my back, mess up my hair, or play-
punch me, like they would
anybody else,

All because the magical touch
of a beautiful girl has
turned me into a
somebody.

Crossing the Line

Annabelle

Mr. Dawe is in trouble for pushing us into the mall.
The administration rapped his knuckles for crossing
a line between *teaching us about the world*
and *interfering in the community.*

They told him it's okay to organize booths
at school, but gathering with students at malls,
then harassing people inside those malls,
is *way beyond* the teacher's code of conduct.

Mr. Dawe disagrees. He says learning doesn't stop
at the school gates. It's *everywhere,* and what better place
to learn about the warped values of consumer society
than at the mall—the modern day town square?

We all agree with him
and want to start a petition,
but since we are only seven
members, it seems *hopeless.*

Mr. Dawe says not to worry. He has *no intention*
of slowing down. Rome wasn't built in a day
and if all the makers and shakers of history had quit
so easily, there would have been no progress.

Believe it or not, our flyers
are as powerful as stones or bullets.
They can help change the world,
one thought at a time.

All I Need to Know
Stacey

Mark drives the Mini over bridges,
    the water under us
    frozen and gray.

We pass sleepy summer towns,
    boarded up
    and hibernating.

The roads are lined with trees,
    tall and stiff
    as exclamation marks.

Mark's face is completely closed,
    his peppery stubble
    dark and scratchy.

Way behind us, the rehearsal
    is on, which means
    I'm off the show.

On the back seat, my homework
    lies untouched, my
    marks are falling fast—

And in my mind the memory
    of Mark's affection
    is fading faster.

Back home, my parents
    are angry, begging
    me to stay home.

Ahead of us, the mountains
    are folded over,
    brown and angry.

Under me, my fingers are crossed
    as I pray we
    won't drive up them.

Telling Annabelle

Christopher

How can I tell
Annabelle

That, in a way,
I agree

With the school
about not crossing

The line
into the mall?

Mr. Dawe says
our flyers

Are as powerful
as bullets

But do people
like my aunt

Really deserve
to get shot?

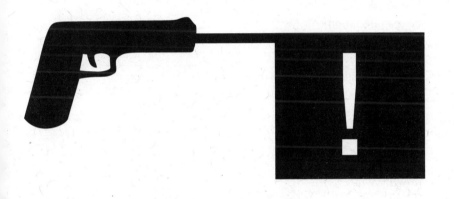

Appassionata
With passion
Mary

Two more weeks now
before the show.

Late night, all-dressed
pizza supper,

Ten extra-large
boxes piled high,

Got to join in
can't hold back.

Make-up, costumes,
dress-rehearsal,

White silky shirt,
flowing white skirt,

Foundation, blush,
mascara,

Stacey's replace-
ment stepping up.

In the mirror
a stranger stands,

Lipstick smile,
unfamiliar:

Me, but not me,
new me, old me.

Joining in, as
best I can, part-

icipating,
zipping dresses,

Encouraging
words, *break a leg.*

My turn, the light
circles around

the piano
like an island.

A flock of birds
flutters inside.

My *debut con-
cert recital.*

Don't think
too hard, just walk

Composed, on high
heels, straight to

The bench, con-
fident, expert,

Sitting straight-backed
inhale, exhale,

Let it come, with-
out thought. Instinct

Taking over,
years of training,

Memory, my
best friend, music,

My calling, my
passion, my joy.

Heresy
Christopher

Now, when I
think of
you,

alone
in my room
at night,

I wish I had
a telescope
that

could see through
space and
time

straight to
where you
are.

Galileo
used his
own

to prove the
sun was the
centre

of the universe
and got locked
up

for heresy. Would
it be heresy
now

if I could prove
that everything
inside me

turns
around
you?

As a Dad
Annabelle

It funny to think that Christopher
is the same age
as my father was
when he fathered me.

I try to picture Christopher as a dad,
pushing a stroller,
changing a diaper,
playing *this little piggy*,

All the things my father never did
with me, because
he *never even knew*
that I'd been born.

I wonder if it's as strange for him
as it is for me, not knowing
what I look like
or who I am, but

It can't be. Since he doesn't
know about me, he doesn't
scan the faces of sixteen-
year-old girls, hoping to find me.

It must have been hard
for my mom to hide
being pregnant
from my father.

Even though he didn't go to her school,
he'd still have been around town,
at movies, or restaurants,
or the park.

Did she jump behind mailboxes or
into stores to avoid him, or did
she just walk by and *pretend*
not to know him?

She told me she barely knew him
so maybe she didn't need to
hide, maybe he wouldn't
have recognized her.

If so, the big bump in her belly was
nothing to him, a meaningless
shape, something he'd
look right past.

That scenario bothers me the most.
I prefer to picture him stopping
and staring, his mouth
falling open,

His conscience prickling him,
every thought in his head
turning toward the
reality of *me*,

There inside my mother's womb,
curled up sucking my little
thumb, my face already
resembling his.

Stiracchiando
Holding back
Mary

I don't know where it
came from,

This ability to play,
maybe

From a recessive gene
hidden

Way back in the family
pool.

My parents are not musical—
my dad

Barely taps his toes to
music

And my mom is
tone deaf.

Maybe that's why she thinks
I can

Turn it on
on command,

Like she's the organ
grinder

and I'm her faithful
monkey,

Penny in the slot and here
we go.

But it's not that
simple.

The music stirs in-
side me

Almost like a chick
tapping

On its shell when it's
ready

To emerge, its eyes closed
against

The starkness of the light,
like me

Up on the stage at school
first time.

When people want to pull
music

Out of me it makes me
angry

Because the music is part
of me,

It's not detachable, like a
fake limb.

Something She Doesn't Know
Annabelle

I see the way Stacey stares at me
and Christopher like she a) *can't
believe* I have a boyfriend and b)
can't believe it's Christopher.

Sometimes, I see her
whisper to her pack
and they giggle
and look over.

But other times, when she's alone,
I catch her looking another
way, like she's trying to
figure something out.

It might be because Christopher
can't take his eyes off me,
or his hands, both are always
touching me, circling me,

While Mark is never near her
anymore, not like before
when they were like vines,
constantly entwined. Now

He jerks like he wants
to shake her loose, like
snow from branches
or flies from food.

She cracks up when he does it
like it's funny, while Mark's dark
eyes stare dead ahead, like she's
nowhere in his line of vision.

Once he left, leaving her looking
like a fool, her arm in mid-air,
like a character in a sci-fi film
whose partner's been sucked away.

Part of me wanted to laugh, but
I was sorry for her too, especially
when she had to shrug
and act like it didn't matter.

THE KEY

Mark

This time,
I brought the spare key
for my father's cab.

I thought if I buried it on the land
he loved so much, it would be
like he was finally here, living
the life he wanted,

Hiking in the woods
fishing in the stream,
breathing deep to fill his lungs
with mountain air, opening
his arms to embrace space,
the thing he wanted more than anything,

Maybe more than me because I did nothing
but make his space smaller, shrinking it
with anger, filling it
with words my cousins in Lebanon
would never use with *their* father.

The key slides under the rock
and the cold metal turns hot
in my fingers, as if
the earth has been warming up
like an oven to receive it.

The only thing that ruins it is Stacey
waiting in the car, cold and cranky,
expecting me to share something with her,
cursing me, making me feel like
the world's worst screw-up boyfriend.

The guys at school think we drive out to do it
because Stacey's so hot. They think
I can have her whenever, wherever I want,
that there is nothing to stop me.

Nothing except my father's voice describing
the girl of his dreams for me: someone
sweet and pure who wants nothing more
than a home in the suburbs and two kids,
who'll go to church on Sundays, keep
my house sparkling clean and make roast
lamb when he and my mom come to visit.

Back Again
Stacey

When I recognized the road,
twisting, snow-topped,
my heart stopped.

Mark didn't even want me to come.
He told me to stay at rehearsal,
but I couldn't let him go

                    without me

because I knew if
I did it would be
over because he

already had that far
away look in his eyes,
telling me he wanted to be

                  alone.

He parked the same place
as last time, by a pile of logs
marking the dead end of the road

and without a word
disappeared into the trail,
shoulders hunched,

                  determined.

Two whole hours I sat in the car
freezing, rubbing my hands together,
wondering what the hell I was doing

tagging along on this mad journey
to nowhere with some guy who's
obviously going completely

crazy

When I could be doing hair and makeup,
stuff I'm good at, instead of sitting here
like a fifth wheel in some little car

in the woods, wondering what would happen
if Mark never returned and nobody even knew
where I was, leaving me completely

stranded.

Pregnant
Annabelle's Mom

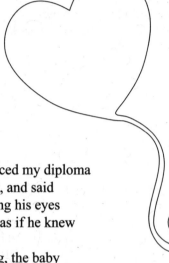

At graduation, the Principal placed my diploma
in my left hand, shook my right, and said
"All the best in the future," fixing his eyes
somewhere around my middle, as if he knew

My future was in there, growing, the baby
already eight weeks old, with eyes of its own,
toes and fingers and a tiny heart
beating, beating, beating.

I knew his words didn't mean studies
and career, but diapers and cracked nipples,
things that terrified me and had me
teetering in indecision,

Unsure of what I was going to do,
my whole body numb, as though
what was going on inside me
had turned me completely dumb.

Months later, still small enough to hide
my bump, I felt the first flutter
of baby kick, like a fish flicking
in the glass bowl of my belly

And I jumped, knocking the bowl
of popcorn off my lap, spilling
its contents onto the floor,
like an omen of bigger spills to come.

My mom listened without a word of reproach,
she knew the gods had conspired to make love
hard for girls and easier for boys, who were
let off the hook the minute the deed was done,

But my dad crumpled, as though a giant crane
had dropped a concrete block
on his head, his whole body collapsing
under the weight of the news.

In the end it was just the three of us,
me, my mom and Annabelle, a chain
of girls, harmonious even through
night feedings and early changes,

My mom pitching in like a trooper,
loving every talcum-powdered moment
in a way I'm not sure I would if that
were to happen now with Annabelle.

So Perfect
Annabelle

Last night my mom told me that when I was a baby
she would bring me to the park and sit
in the shade while I slept.

The older moms would stare and whisper,
trying to figure out if she was the mom
or the sitter.

She couldn't join in their talk
about feeding and sleeping
and changing.

She had to hide me, when every bone in her body
wanted to lift me up and show me off
to the world.

At home she couldn't stop looking at me, wondering
how she'd made something
so perfect,

When even her simple grad dress
with the braided straps had
stumped her.

I know why she told me this story.

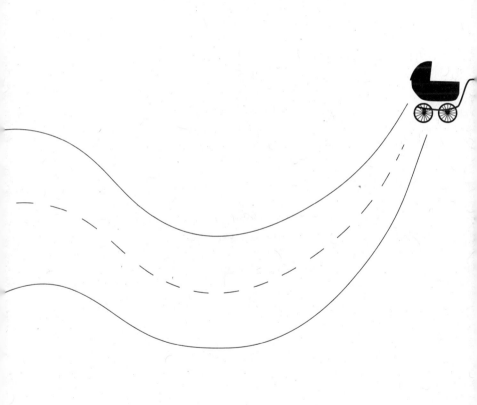

LOST
Stacey's Dad

One daughter already lost
>to the west coast:
>rocky mountains
>grizzly bears
>avalanches
>crazy cults.

The other is here but:
>running wild
>faking nice
>skipping school
>going nowhere
>breaking my heart.

In my wallet is a picture of:
>both together
>matching dresses
>licking ice cream
>moustache smiles
>simpler times.

I'm getting too old for all this:
>
> worrying
> regretting
> fretting
> sweating
> pretending.

I just want to coast into old age:
>
> quietly
> gracefully
> comfortably
> easily
> peacefully.

Instead of wondering if I was too:
>
> permissive
> disconnected
> undisciplined
> inattentive
> much to blame.

Deck The Halls

Annabelle

Christmas is the *best* time
        to make our point,
Christmas is the *worst* time
        to make our point.

People shop and shop and we try
        to stop them
and make them *think* about what
        they're buying.

Christopher wears a Santa hat
        and rings a bell
to pull them over, like he's
        part of the scene.

Up close they see his *Santa's little helper*
        button, showing a dark kid
stuffing a bear that also wears
        a Santa hat.

Mr. Dawe thought it was an *awesome*
        scheme. He likes the way
our minds are becoming devious
        and subversive.

I like the way Mr. Dawe is not a teacher
        we have to obey
but another person handing out flyers
        to dumb shoppers.

I like the way he's willing to take
        this chance and go
against the administration by taking
        us to the mall.

Last meeting, he told us about a conference
        on youth and fashion,
called *No Your Clothes*, right in the heart
        of New York City.

Our group is going to fundraise and take
        the bus to Manhattan
where we'll stay in the dorms of NYU
        near Washington Square.

We'll do workshops by day and sightsee at night.
        It sounds great, but
I don't know if my mom will let me go,
        even if we do raise the money.

Mr. Dawe says I'm *old enough* to make up
        my own mind, eighteen
is an arbitrary age and in the middle ages I'd be
        married by now.

I looked at Christopher when he said that
        and felt myself blush
as I pictured us fooling around in a haystack,
        husband and wife.

BACK AGAIN

Mark

Back down
>   from the
>   mountains.

Back here
>   on familiar streets
>   looking for
>   familiar faces.

Back where
>   I suppose I belong,
>   even though these days
>   I don't feel like I belong
>   anywhere except in my car.

Back when
>   I was a kid I didn't think
>   much about things like that.
>   I just sort of lived day to day
>   doing kid stuff like soccer
>   and hockey and school projects.

Back then
>it all seemed easier, like there were
>no cracks in my life, no places where
>my feet kept slipping through, like
>they do now whenever I try to take a step,
>whenever I try to decide how I am going
>to move forward in my life and not

Backwards
>like I am now, constantly thinking
>of things that happened in the past,
>things with my dad, like the time he
>let me stay home from school and spend
>the day with him in his cab and we couldn't
>let on to my mom because she'd have flipped,
>especially if she knew that he let me drive the car

Back to
>the depot, even though I was only twelve
>and barely tall enough to see over the steering
>wheel or to reach the gas and brakes, although
>it was only two blocks in mid-afternoon so there
>weren't many other cars on the road, and it was so
>exciting and I couldn't wait to brag about it to my
>friends at school and every day after that when my mom
>wasn't in sight, I'd beg and beg my dad to take me

Back again.

WHO IS THIS
Christopher's Father

Young
man, suddenly
tall and confident,
singing in the shower,
eager out the door, not held
back, reluctant, like he used to be
to face the world, one shoulder always
slightly behind the other as though he was
hesitating, his chin down, his eyes staring out
from under his bangs, watching, waiting for the shower
of taunts and insults that he was sure would come his way the
minute his foot left the threshold of home, in a way that used to make
me want to run out ahead of him and blast a safe path between our home and
the school, but of course I never could because that is not how fatherhood works?

False

Christopher

I felt stupid in that
Santa hat.

I hated ringing the bell
and luring people over
on false pretences.

I know it's for a good cause
but it's Annabelle's
cause—not mine.

It took me a while
to figure that out
but I know it now.

Some of the guys saw me
and they were laughing
between the double doors.

They were ringing invisible bells,
doubled over, *hohoho*-ing
and punching each other.

The awful thing was
that I wanted
to join them.

I wanted to rip off the hat
and run inside and be with them,
like old times.

Will Annabelle still want
to be with me if I tell her
I want to stop?

Will she think I'm scum
if she finds out I joined up
just to meet her?

IT MUST HAVE BEEN

Mark

Someone else with Stacey

down the highway

full speed full volume

her hand on his thigh

him on, his right hand

the shift to keep from

as she stroked higher

the gas to keep them

down the road

to go on that way

riding

flying

singing

turning

clutching

falling

pressing

zooming

wanting

forever.

Volante
Taking flight
Mary

Only days to go until the show
  and even though I no longer seize up
    when I sit at the piano, the thought
      of playing to a packed house still
        makes my stomach flutter like a bunch
          of butterflies, trapped and desperate
            for escape, colliding and tumbling, wings breaking,
              making every bone in my fingers
            shake and my mouth turn dry as dust
          until all I can do to quell the fear is picture
        the wings becoming whole and the insects
      soaring, light and breezy, into the sky
    making me feel calm and ready to play.

Adventure
Annabelle

I'm going to New York
     whether my Mom likes it
        or not.

It's my turn now to grab
     the world by its string
        and fly,

To leave this sleepy place behind
     and have a real ad-
        venture

On streets packed with people:
     Times Square, Central Park
        Soho.

I want to live in the world of
     ideas and action,
        sleeves up,

Ready to pitch in, high
     on belief and hope
        and love.

Mr. Dawe says ideals are
     what fuelled his gener-
        ation

To protest the war in
        Vietnam and gain rights
                for Blacks.

He says only certain
        people understand
                ideals

Because they can't be bought cheap
        and plastic-wrapped at
                the mall.

You have to have them inside
        you, rooted deep, like
                a heart.

He says I'll be like Alice, falling
        through the rabbit hole,
                landing

In the Big Apple, eyes
        wide, hungry, eager
                to bite.

The Big
Christopher

BANG

I told her
I want to go
to New York

But not so much to learn
about the evils
of fashion.

I want to visit the
Hayden Planetarium
where the Zeiss Star

Projector can take us back
to the Big Bang,
where it all began.

I picture Annabelle in the evenings
beside me, looking up,
her perfect neck

An archway to the heavens,
where the sun
will swell

And explode
Five billion years
in the future.

But, judging by the way
her face fell
when I confessed to her,

I don't think
that's ever
going to happen.

Going Through the Motions
Annabelle

I thought he wanted
     the same things I want.

I thought we were two minds
     thinking one thing:

How the world has got
     to change. But it turns out

His mind is fixated on
     how the world was made.

The workshop on *logos*
     and how they invade our space

Didn't turn him on
     like I thought it would.

He'd rather study *outer space*
     and the symbols in the sky.

And the workshop on *stars*
     and how they sell brands

Didn't mean as much to him as
     real stars and how they burn.

When we said goodbye, I wondered
      if *everything* between us

Was an illusion, if when Christopher
      handed out flyers

He was just going
      through the motions

Like someone in a sandwich board
      selling hotdogs or pop or fries.

For the first time,
      I didn't want to kiss him.

And when he called me later
      I just let it ring.

ALL AROUND ME

Mark

I feel her all around me
               all the time,
       her arms like tentacles
her voice, nails on the blackboard.

I used to want her
             beside me,
       her legs across the stick
shift, pearl white from skirt to boot.

When she turned toward me
             they parted and I could see
       the dark space between them, as
inviting as that cave my dad once found.

It was inside the mountain, smelling
             of damp earth, its floor
                 a carpet of pine needles
stretching way back into the rock.

We packed *tabouli* and *pita*,
             chips and Coke,
       and spent the day pretending
to be shipwrecked.

We were pirates, marooned
             on a desert island far
       from home, surviving on
next to nothing, beating the odds

Until my mom came calling,
                    clashing pots to scare
            the bears into the hills,
and made us come home.

Then he carried me across
                    his shoulders
            to the cottage that smelled
of wet wood and smoke

and lay me on the bottom bunk,
                    so soft I sank
            to the floor, dreaming
of marshmallows.

Now, I want that kind of sleep
                    to take me away,
            a thousand leagues away
from my life, far away

from Stacey and my mom and school, all
                    constantly wanting
            things from me that I
cannot give.

Everywhere I turn someone is
                    expecting,
            taking grabbing plucking
at my life.

Can't they see that I'm like an
                    empty tank
            running on nothing
but fear?

Cuddling Up
Stacey

I've decided to focus on the talent show.
      Even though I'm no longer
            in charge, I'm keen

To pitch in somehow, leave my mark
      on as many faces
            as possible.

I'm determined to do
      Mary's make-up.
            I don't know why

But driving home the other night,
      Mark dark as a demon
            beside me,

The only thing that kept me sane
      was her song running
            through my brain,

Filling the spaces left by Mark's
      wacko walk
            into the woods.

He didn't say one word the whole trip home,
      then dropped me off
            like a package.

I tiptoed up the creaky stairs,
        past my parents' bedroom,
                light but heavy.

I wanted to shout them awake
        and tell them how Mark had treated
                their daughter.

I pictured myself crawling between
        them, burrowing against
                their warm bodies

Like I used to when I was sick
        or scared awake
                by a nasty dream.

But of course I didn't—couldn't—
        because those kid days
                are gone.

Instead, I crawled into bed
        and nestled deep between
                the sheets, nothing

But the moon for comfort
        as I cried myself
                to sleep.

RUST
Mark

I'm going back to check out the key, to see
if the earth has swallowed it, pulled it into
the soil that was as mushy as quicksand.

I'm bringing some plastic wrap to cover it
before putting it back, to coat it and protect it
so that it won't turn to rust.

That's what's bugging me, the thought
of the shiny key turning orangey-brown
then flaking away in bits and pieces.

I've been wondering how long it would take
for a brass key to decompose. That's not
something we learned at school because they

Only teach us useless stuff, like the symbols
for elements, not stuff we need to know like whether
oxidization takes place inside the earth.

I want this key to stay shiny and new
so that I can come back here when I'm older,
like someone on an archaeological dig,

Looking for clues of some long lost
civilization, only in this case it would be
the civilization of my father.

I'm going to stay all night, like I'm on a field trip
or maybe even two nights if that's how long it takes
to make sure I'm doing things right this time.

This could be one of those strange initiation rituals
where boys go into the woods and build huts
and talk to the stars or hunt wild boars,

Or maybe a vision quest, where guys hang out
in the trees and wait for a voice to speak to them
telling them what to do and who they'll be.

My voice would be my father's, its soft tone
and hard accent mixing me up, telling me to pull
myself together, just like he used to.

Gravity
Christopher

For months I did her thing
      and it was my thing too,

Maybe not as much,
      but I believed in it too

Because even before I met her
      I thought the world was dumb.

Why can't she see that there's more
      than one way to look for meaning?

Annabelle thinks words
      can change the world

And maybe she's right,
      but does she know

It took only three minutes to create
      all the matter there has ever been?

That it took less than a second
      for gravity to appear?

That we can still hear the buzz
      of cosmic radiation, 90 billion trillion miles away?

I think if people knew
      these bigger things

They'd realize it's crazy
       to kill yourself for fashion.

That's all I was trying to tell her
       but she shut me out

Like my opinion wasn't
       as important as hers.

When she turned her face away
       from my kiss, it made me feel heavy,

Like a field of gravity
       had invaded my limbs.

COURAGE
Mary's Dad

We say a little prayer
       while walking
              to the school,
not because we're hoping
       she'll be a star,
              but because we hope
she'll end the night
       feeling good
              about her first time on
stage.

It'll be
       a defining moment
              in her young life,
one she'll draw on
       whenever she needs
              strength or courage,
and god knows we all
       need lots of each
              to get through
life.

When she was born
       I held her, sweet
              pink bundle,
little gush of baby breath
       the grip of baby finger,
              the tiny delicate bone,
her blue eyes
       flickering
              and I was instantly in
love.

I hope she'll
          feel us
                    out there
in the crowd,
          sending her
                    our warmth,
watching her
          play the piano
                    like only we know she
can.

Intrepidezza
Without fear
Mary

___

Overture, curtains, lights,
This is it, the night of nights . . .

Mostly off-key, we all sing it
        together
        in a circle
        holding hands.
It's kind of hokey, but
        for the first time
        in my life
        I feel part of
something bigger than me
        and my circle
        of light in
        the basement.

When we yell *break a leg*
        upwards
        to the ceiling
        to the lights
I can't believe one of the voices
        mingling
        with the rest
        is mine.

And when Stacey dabs
        white on my cheeks
        silver on my lids
        and on my lips

I can't believe she doesn't
        sneer
        or grunt
        with disgust.

And when I wait in the back room that's
        electric
        with energy
        and excitement
I can't believe it's me kids turn to
        for advice on hair
        or clothes
        or courage,
like they're seeing me as
        someone new,
        someone even I
        don't recognize
when I look in the full-length mirror
        that reflects
        this transformed
        about-to-perform me.

Mary's Music
Annabelle

I tell Mr. Dawe I'll have to leave our booth in the lobby,
with all our pamphlets and cupcakes and cookies,
when Mary is on and he doesn't say no
because he's not big
on authority.

Mary comes out, dressed in white, gliding
to the piano that sits in a circle
of light, the lid open
like an archway
above
her.

She sits still for a few
minutes, as if she is
frozen, then her
hands rise
over the
keys.

At first, the music is soft,
staying on the stage,
then slowly it rolls
out, over the
crowd, like
fog.

Suddenly, we are surrounded
by Mary's music, the notes
flowing between us
around us and
inside us.

When she stops, we all want to clap
but hesitate, as if it would be too
rude to cut into the music that
keeps resonating long
after Mary has
left the
stage.

I float my way back to our booth,
its top filled with flyers
about ugly things,

And for a long time I don't
want to look
down.

Lights

Christopher

When I'm at the board
I feel

Like I'm master of a
universe,

Each slider and switch
a star

That I oversee, like
Galileo.

I promised Annabelle
I'd give

Mary the greatest light
of all,

And I think I fulfilled
that promise.

But will Annabelle give me
any credit?

Empty
Mark's Mom

Staring at your empty bed,
I think of the day
your cat died.

You fell asleep hugging
the hot water bottle
to your chest.

In the morning, I emptied it,
the water pumping out
like a beating heart.

Now, wondering where
you are, my heart
gushes the same way

Emptying, leaving me
full of nothing
but fear.

What are you doing
out there, alone
in your crazy car?

All night—no return
no phone call
no sign of life.

If your father could see
what you are doing to me,
he would kill you,

But that's exactly
what you may be doing
to yourself.

Ideals
Annabelle

My mom stops at our booth
during Intermission.

I watch the way her eyes glance
over the pamphlets

Like she doesn't really want
to take them in

But then one catches her eye:
Carpet Weaving.

And I wonder if it's because she's always
going on about carpets,

How they can make or break a sale
in someone's home.

I watch her open it and read about
Iqbal Masih,

A carpet weaver in Pakistan who started
working at age four

Ran away at ten, then was shot and killed
at twelve.

She stands and reads it for a long time,
her face growing red

As she learns how he risked his life
by talking

About the evils of bonded labour
all over the world.

When she's finished, she tucks it into
her purse,

Turns to Mr. Dawe, shakes his hand
and thanks him

For all the wonderful work
he is doing.

I just about fall of my chair because
I remember

Her saying that ideals don't pay
the rent.

Now, I wonder if, when she's walking
strangers

Through beautiful homes, her high heels
echoing

off the ceilings like trapped birds,
her mind

Does wander to other things; if, when she's
smiling and quoting

Prices on new roofs and marble counter tops
her mind

Does wonder about things she can't afford
to dwell on

Because she has to make that sale:
it's how we eat.

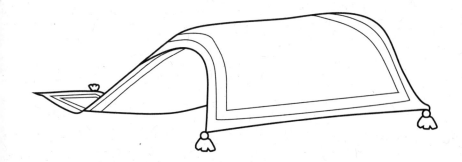

First Time

Mary's Mom

Watching the show, I finally got it:
your ability to shut everything out.

Tonight, I stopped fighting
your piano and just
listened.

For once, I was inside your music,
instead of outside,
wanting in.

Tonight I could see that your playing
has nothing to do
with me

That playing the piano is not something
you are doing
to me.

It is entirely yours, completely separate
from anything I can
control.

Super Charged

Annabelle

I sneak back inside during
a dance number.

Christopher's lights are bouncing
off the dancer's feet—

Yellow and blue, with streaks
of silver on the back wall.

I think of the show Christopher
described at the Planetarium.

He wants to spend both evenings there
under the galaxy

Watching the universe
dance across the dome

Instead of sitting in diners
with me and the others, like I pictured,

The two of us *leaning close*,
planning to change the world.

His face in the booth is super-charged,
smiling wide above the board

Like I've never seen him smile
near the stores

And I wonder if I was wrong
to expect him to want

The same things
as me.

BIG WHITE SMILE
Mark

The Mini's high beams are not very strong,
       but they're all I've got to steer me off
              this road and onto the highway.

Branches grab the car like claws
       that want to catch me and take me
              hostage deep inside the woods.

Owls hoot and wolves howl
       like the whole forest is pissed
              off that I am here, intruding.

I knew it was time to go when the clouds cleared,
       uncovering a crescent moon that hung
              like a big white smile in the sky.

My dad's key was shiny in the ground
       at my feet and I could almost feel his hand
              squeezing my shoulder, saying thanks.

Control

Christopher

I thought I might have blown my chance of being
in New York
in love with
Annabelle

    My dad gave me the talk on
    respecting
    her body
    and my own,

    Like I don't have any self-control
    and will pounce
    the minute
    we're alone.

    Still, when I pictured the two of us
    late at night
    temptation
    closing in,

It was hard not to think about
undressing
caressing
messing with

Annabelle. I thought I lost her by
revealing
my real
intentions,

But when she looked up at the booth
it struck me
hard – like a
ray of hope.

Eclipse
Stacey

It worked like
I knew it would:
      Mary all in
      white
      like the full moon
            that was the only thing
            keeping me company
            last week in the woods.

No one knew
I did it.
      It's not like
      I could hang
      a sign
            around her neck
            for everyone to see:
            designed by Stacey.

Especially
for my parents
      who were sitting
      out there watching,
      looking sad
            because they weren't sure
            I was backstage
            working.

It's not like
I could announce
       where I was going,
       suddenly
       keeping them
             informed
             and in the loop
             of my life.

They always look
so lost,
       like my sister's leaving
       turned their smiles
       upside down
             and nothing I have done
             has helped to flip them
             right side up again.

I wonder if
they'll look that way
       forever now, never
       laughing, never
       light-hearted,
             always heavy
             always hurting
             always wondering

Why their daughters
were so hard
        to raise and
        didn't seem
        to give a shit
                about anyone
                else's feelings
                but their own.

Sometimes
I think if
        they would just smile more,
        forget my sister and focus
        on here and now,
                show some sign
                of wanting
                to be happy

I'd come round
and spend time
        with them, instead
        of always running
        as far away as I can
                to escape their sadness,
                their shrugged shoulders
                and their brick-like guilt.

When the crew
takes a bow
     I look right into
     their eyes,
     our first contact
          in ages,
          to show them
          I am here.

That's when I see their
smiles, slight but there,
     and I know the reason
     they came was
     to try to see me,
          like a rare
          eclipse
          of the sun.

Trionfale

Triumphant

Mary

Chopin knew he'd done well
when he could say

That he had played as he played
when he was alone.

Tonight, I think I can say
just that.

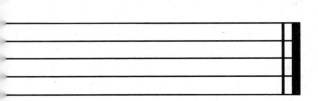

Fine

Relief
Stacey's Mom

Tonight reminded me
        of school concerts
when she was little and
        full of bounce

Up on stage, twirling and
        bursting with song,
the fastest reindeer, the
        the brightest star

And I would think, *that's my*
        girl, sprung from me
with such perfection in
        every cell.

I'd be the first to leap
        to my feet for
for the standing O, blowing
        her kisses.

Tonight I didn't stand,
        but I was caught
by the beam of her eyes
        piercing mine.

Relief flooded through me
        just to know she
was safe and not roaming
        in that car

No bigger than a bug,
        no protection
in a crash, no escaping
        her boyfriend.

I could feel her dad
        caught beside me,
pulling pictures from his
        memory,

Opening them slowly,
        holding his breath,
as though he was scared of
        what he'd see.

Syncopation
Unexpected emphasis on weak beats

Mary

I can go to the
cast party now,
because I am one of
the gang.

I don't need to turn
my shoulders in
and shy away from
people.

Even if I just sit
in a corner and watch
the action and absorb
the fun

I'll still be okay,
because people look at me
differently now, not
the same

As before when they
didn't know me,
didn't know my
music

And just saw me as
some weirdo who never
talked or played
the game

That everyone my age
       is supposed to play:
              pretending and posing,
                     the art

Of making yourself
       someone who everyone
              else wants to get to know,
                     the way

Stacey does, like a pro,
       although tonight she seemed
              different, not her usual
                     loud self.

She even asked me
       to wait up for her so we
              could walk together to the
                     party,

Which made me look
       around, like maybe
              I didn't get
                     the joke,

But there was no one around,
       just the two of us in the hallway,
              eerily quiet and still after
                     the show.

Hope
Annabelle

They walk off, practically *holding hands*,
Stacey *breathing* down Mary's neck,

Like Mary is suddenly her *closest friend*
and not someone she likes to call

Roly-poly freak girl
whenever she gets the chance.

I want to follow them, hide
behind trees and mailboxes

Like Nancy Drew, girl detective,
but I can't because I have to help

Mr. Dawe put away the stuff
from our booth.

I hope the hug I gave Mary
earlier, after the show, will act as a kind of

Suit of armour, keeping her *safe* when Stacey
turns back into herself.

I was hoping Christopher would drop by
but *why* would he?

I didn't exactly make him think
I *wanted* him to.

I hope the look I gave Christopher earlier,
before the show, won't act as kind of

Shield, keeping him *away*
from me.

Empty
Christopher

We didn't make plans
to meet

But I go look for Annabelle after the
clean up

Once all our gear is locked
away.

The info booth is
empty,

Nothing remains, not even a
pamphlet

Or petitition or
cupcake

All the things she worked so
hard on.

The bare table in the
dark hall

Reminds me how
I'd feel

Without her in
my life.

Strepitoso
Noisy, boisterous

Mary
___

Wood-paneled
basement
beer boxes
filling
with empties
pool-table
shaking
music
pounding
laughing
buzzing
smoky
corners
bodies
on stairs
screams
outside
more bodies
squeezing in
less and less space
less and less air
firecrackers
exploding
doors
slamming
kids
crying
floating by
Stacey vanished

and suddenly
I want
to be
above ground
where there's
air and space
and no
noise or
people

Only me
myself
and I.

I tried this scene
but it's
definitely
not mine.

EXPERIENCE

Mr. Dawe

These kids are
ready, eager
for meaning.

I could see it
in the way
they ran the booth

And sold the treats
to raise money
during the show.

New York won't
disappoint,
how could it?

It's got every-
thing, the whole
world in one.

It'll set them
free, unleash
their young minds.

Experience
is all, nothing
else matters.

Their parents are
scared, I
can see that.

It's the news
on TV, always
negative.

Focusing on
drugs, shootings
street violence.

What about the
rest—art, music,
poetry?

All the devoted
people, working
for justice?

That's what I'll show
these kids, give
them a taste

Of what's going
on, every day
in New York.

The world needs
hope—these
kids are mine.

Good Intentions
Stacey

I want to be there for her, at least
        that's what I pictured
                in my mind,

But when we get here
        and she just kind of freezes
                against the wall

Like she is having some kind
        of panic attack,
                her eyes wide,

A spastic smile
        glued to her face,
                all my good

Intentions fly outside
        and I follow them
                up the stairs and out the door

Where I find some people to hang with
        and drink a few beers and
                smoke some joints

And have a good time like
        any normal person does
                at a party.

At one point, when I have to pee,
    I pass her, still glued
        to the wall

Like she is waiting for me to return
    like I said I would and be
        her best friend.

I don't want to, but I catch the
    deer-in-the-headlights look
        in her eyes

And it makes me think of my dad
    when I came out to bow
        at curtain call

And his eyes caught mine, hard,
    like the beam of a cop's
        flashlight,

Making me feel like a criminal because
    I know he thinks I have stolen
        his little girl.

When he smiled, his eyes softening,
    it sent a zap right through
        my body

Like he'd reached in and stunned
        my heart with some kind of
                electric rod.

I know he'd want me
        to go to Mary and be nice
                and rescue her

Because that's how he always saw me,
        as someone who always did
                the right thing,

Because up until last year, before that swim
        out to the big rock with Paul,
                I always did.

Both Things
Annabelle

I'm not really invited
to the party

But I came to look
for Christopher.

I want to tell him
we can do *both things,*

Workshops and Planetarium:
my thing and his, *together.*

I was also hoping
to find Mary

But this house is
crazy crowded

And I can't find
anyone I know

Except Stacey
who is outside

Cracking up
Like a hyena.

I watch her
stumble away

A six-pack
under her arm

And I wonder
if she's okay.

THE SHAPE

Mark

I'm driving the streets, thinking of crashing
the cast party, except Stacey
will be there, totally
pissed off

At me and the last thing I need is someone
bringing me down when I'm still
feeling pretty
high

From what went on back there, up
in the mountains, my dad's
key now locked
up safe.

Idling my Mini outside the house, I let
my heart syncopate with the beat
of the music banging
the brick,

And I picture all the stuff going on inside
those walls: the beer, the girls,
the pool, the music,
the fun

But I can't decide if I want to go in or not. It's like
my old self is in there, waiting for me
to become the life of the
party

But I don't know how to take this new self
in there and pick up where I
left off, like nothing
has changed.

Suddenly this shape floats outside, straight
across the yard, caught by the low
beam of my Mini's
park-lights.

It looks like a ghost, white from head to toe,
and I wonder if it will walk right
through me, like ghosts do
on TV.

Maybe I shouldn't have spent a whole night alone
in the woods, thinking about my dead
father and hearing his voice
in my head.

It's made me see things weird, on top of
filling my nails with dirt
and coating my teeth
with moss.

I'm just about to hit the gas and take off when
the shape turns towards me
and I see that it's
her,

That girl who plays the piano like she's in a trance
and never talks to anyone except
that do-gooder girl I see
at the mall.

I hear Stacey's voice in my ear calling her a freak
because that's how Stacey is, always
running people down with her
fast tongue,

Which is something I used to like about her
because it suited the image
my souped-up Mini
gave me.

Tonight I do something I never thought
I would do: I open the door
and yell at piano girl to
get in.

She's the last girl I ever thought I'd see in my car
and I don't even look at her for a while
because I know she won't
look right.

She'll be as out of place as I feel
just about everywhere
in the world
right now.

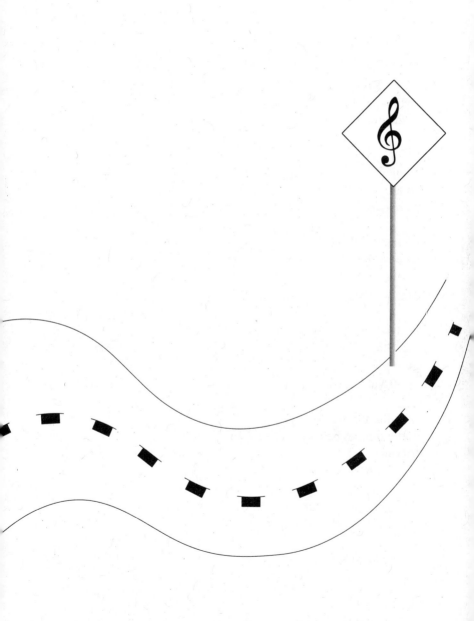

Counterpoint

Rhythmically different but harmonically intertwined

Mary

My fingers tap
a two-beat rhythm,
echoing
in the quiet car.

Mark's fingers drum
counterpoint,
creating
an odd effect.

I wonder if he's doing it
on purpose, to avoid
having
to talk to me,

If he regrets that I'm in the seat
that Stacey usually occupies,
giving
us all the finger.

If I told him what she did to me,
pretending to be nice then
leaving
me on my own,

Would he laugh and call
me pathetic for
being
such a loser?

I'm thinking I should just open
the door and leave,
letting
him off the hook,

When Mark does something
totally unexpected,
making
me wonder

If everything I think about people
is wrong and they're just
faking
most of the time,

Because next thing I know he
is looking at me sweetly,
asking
me where I live.

Smoking Weed
Stacey

Makes me feel fuzzy,
like I am not
really there

So I can't really care whether
Mark is with me
or not.

It doesn't matter because
there's a cottony
zone

Around me, with no sharp
edges, nothing
brittle

for me to bump against,
or cut me, just
soft space

That I slide into, forgetting
how much so many
things hurt.

Midnight

Mary's Mom

Midnight and it's the first
time she's been out
so late and not at
Annabelle's house.

I'm pacing the floor,
worrying about her
on her own at this party
at a stranger's house.

Midnight and I'm resisting
waking her dad, sending
him out into the dark
to fetch her back.

Midnight and I'm telling
myself to get a grip,
sooner or later
I'll have to let her go.

I'm listening for
the slam
of a taxi door
meaning she's here.

Midnight and a car is pulling
into the driveway,
a guy at the wheel
talking laughing.

I'm hiding
in the curtains, watching
as he leans toward her
still talking.

Midnight and I'm breathing
in fabric dust as she comes
in the door, kicking
off her shoes.

I keep hiding
because I don't know
what to say as she
hums her way upstairs.

Stacey
Annabelle

She is sitting in the yard, plucking dead grass
into a heap near her feet, mascara
streaking her cheeks.

She starts mumbling stuff about Mark and Mary,
about woods and moons, about
waiting in the Mini.

I'm wondering how I'm going to help her home
when Christopher appears, holding
out his hand.

We walk Stacey around the block three times,
making her gulp the cool air before
climbing her stairs.

At the top, her face clears and she says my name,
drawing out its three syllables like she is
remembering

Something from *long ago*, like maybe the time
she got a new puppy and we spent hours
playing with it

Or the day she got her first period and was so scared
that her sister would embarrass her by
telling her dad.

That day, we read the school pamphlet on reproduction
together, marvelling at all the changes
our bodies were going through

Deep down
in the most *secret*
of places.

She looks at Chris, and I wait for her to laugh
or say something mean, but she just nods
and steps inside

Leaving us on the sidewalk, moving close
to fill the space where Stacey's
body once stood.

Surrender
Stacey

All the lights are off
but they don't fool me
because I can feel their
      baited breath.

I know they're awake,
lying still in bed,
thinking to catch me
      drunk or stoned

Even though they won't
call me or come out
because they'd rather
      keep silent

And pretend, like with
my sister, never
facing her head-on
      like parents

In movies do:
yelling and screaming,
demanding answers
      from their kids

Instead of hiding
their heads in the sheets
like they're afraid of
      what they'll see.

What would happen if
I banged and crashed and
stamped my way upstairs
       like thunder,

Noises they couldn't
ignore or pretend
away, forcing them
       to emerge

And smell my beer-breath,
see my blood-shot eyes
and deal with me once
       and for all?

They might be surprised
by how willing I am
to put myself
       in their hands.

THIS GIRL

Mark

I really am going to take her there, this girl
I never spoke to before tonight, this girl
who listened to every word I said about my dad,
who didn't laugh or make feel crazy,
who told me about Chopin,
whose emotions were as raw as a fresh scrape,
who's probably never even kissed a guy,
but plays the piano amazingly, this girl
who is so different and doesn't try to be
someone she isn't, this girl
who is just herself, in a way I'd like to learn to be,
this girl, whose name is
Mary.

Magnetic

Christopher

Walking home from
the party
we can feel
the city
pulling
us in
like a giant
magnet,
our internal
compasses
set
due south
toward
New York.

I picture Annabelle
as Lady Liberty,
raising
her green
torch high
into the air,
her chin tipped
east toward
the ocean,
looking
forward
to changing
people's
lives.

And me?
Will I be like
some poor
immigrant
in the 1920s
looking to her
for
salvation
after a whole day
of gazing
at the sky?

LANDING
Stacey's Dad

I catch her in mid-step
on the upstairs landing
between our bedrooms.

Her foot is raised, frozen
by the click of our door,
like a fawn's paw, caught
by the click of a trigger.

I step up to her, my
arms wide, poised
to catch her like she is
still my little girl.

She is surprised
by my gesture, her body
damp and shivering, not
sure whether to stay or go.

We stand like that
in a deadlock, neither
one moving, until a memory
of contact propels me forward.

She doesn't flinch
when I hug her,
the fight in her melting
away as I stroke her hair,

Her foot finally landing.

What He Did
Stacey

It totally amazes me,
what he did, but why
did it take him so long to do it?

Now I'm wondering, if he'd done
it sooner, to my sister, would she
have stayed home longer?

Maybe she waited months and months
for him to hug her and show her he cared
but nothing happened, so she left.

Maybe, right now, she's waiting
for him to write or call
and ask her to come home.

Maybe she's waiting for all of us
to do something like that, to show
her that we know she's still alive.

I wonder if my mom knew
what my dad was doing while
she was still wrapped up in bed.

Maybe she told him to do it,
because it doesn't seem like
something he'd just do on his own.

Now, lying on my bed, watching
the night turn light, I can still feel
his big hand stroking my hair

And I can still hear his heart
thumping inside his big chest
next to my right ear.

I wish I could send those two things,
his hand and heart, to my sister
so that she could feel them too.

Simplicita
Simplicity

Mary

I crossed over
             tonight
to a place I never
expected to be: inside
             the Yellow Mini,
listening to Mark
talk about
             his dad's death
             and his quest to bury
             his dad's key.

He even showed me
the dirt in his nails,
as if he thought
I wouldn't believe him,
as if it really mattered
             that I did.

Then he said he wanted
to show the spot to
someone and he thought
that someone could be me,
that something about me
made him think
I'd get it
and not laugh
at him or call
him crazy.

The whole time
I was listening
I kept thinking
how strange it was
to be inside
the car
that is normally
reserved
for popular people,
like maybe it was all
a mirage,

Except Mark was real
enough, gripping
the steering wheel,
turning to me,
telling me
          more and more
of his story,
the words pouring out
inside the metal hull,
my ears their only
audience,
like he was performing
a symphony of sorrow
          just for me.

I kept thinking
he'd eventually notice
who he was talking to
and stop and try
to lock his words
back up inside
the tough image
of himself he likes
to project at school,
but he talked
all the way home,
then even more
in the driveway.

When he said that what he did
with the key was weird
but simple, I told him
that Chopin said *Simplicity
is the highest goal.
That's what I strive for
when I play.*

He thanked me
for listening and said he hoped
I'd forget about
what happened
at the party
because shit like that
happens to everyone
and that, in the grand scheme
of things, it didn't really matter.

And the funny thing was,
as I walked into my house
later than ever before,
my mom trying
her best to hide
in the curtains,
like she thought
I'd come home
in a million
pieces,

it suddenly didn't.

Simplicity
Stacey's Mom

It was so simple:
his two arms around
her, forming such a lovely
shape, one that's been captured
in so many ways through the years
in so many famous works of art. As
I watched, I couldn't help thinking how
hugging used to come to us so naturally; we
did it with both girls, and each other, all the time,
yet just now it was like he had to relearn the gesture,
like someone in rehab, learning to walk after an accident.

Into the Adult World

Annabelle's Mom

It's like Annabelle's growth replaced
mine—her limbs, her hair, her ability
to laugh and walk and talk became my
milestones, my own thwarted.

I used to envy the girls I'd graduated
with when I saw them, turning
from girls into women, their newfound
confidence and plans for the future.

They'd coo over Annabelle in her stroller
and, in a way, I knew they envied me,
like they thought I was the one who'd
crossed over into the adult world.

They thought becoming a mother gave me
an automatic ticket, one that let me
bypass all the growing up
they still had to do.

On the outside, I was doing adult things:
shopping for food, banking, arranging daycare,
but inside I was still seventeen, shy, unsure,
stepping timidly outside of myself.

It took me years to make my way
from secretary to agent, baby steps up
the ladder, learning to speak up
and walk like I really belonged.

Now, watching Annabelle pack for New York,
flinging her generic clothes into her bag,
I know it will all be different for her—
nothing will hold her back.

I want to grab her and hold her and tell her
how proud I am of who she is. I did a better job
than I expected. She is stepping out the way
I wish I could have. Part of me will

go with her.

LIGHTENING UP

Mark

Tonight, I don't feel the full
　　　weight of my body
　　　　　when I hit the mattress.
　　　　　　Like before

I buried my dad's key,
　　　I wasn't a body
　　　　　but a torpedo clunking down
　　　　　　ready to explode

And send bits of heavy metal
　　　all over my room
　　　　　and through the walls
　　　　　　to my mom's room

Where she sleeps alone in a king
　　　-sized water bed that must
　　　　　feel wide as an ocean
　　　　　　beside her.

Tonight, I want to wake her up
　　　and show her how light
　　　　　I am, like she could lift
　　　　　　me up herself.

It sounds crazy but I picture
        the two of us doing
                an old-fashioned dance,
                        twirling around,

My hand on her small back,
        steering her away
                from the clutter of stuff
                        we should

Go through one day, things
        like my dad's big oak
                desk under the window,
                        or his stacks

Of *Outdoor Life* magazines
        that are so covered in dust,
                they look exactly like
                        tombstones.

First Step
Annabelle

Sunday night
Packing for New York,
I picture this:

The bus crossing
the Lincoln Tunnel, emerging
into Manhattan, Christopher and me pointing
out the Empire State Building
the Chrysler Building,
and other famous landmarks.

The yellow taxis winding
through busy streets, cutting
through Greenwich Village, taking
us to where the conference is waiting
at NYU.

In the morning,
the store grates scraping,
pigeons cooing,
and cars honking
will wake everyone up and send us hurrying
to our workshops.

In the evening
Christopher and I will be gazing
at stars splashed across the high ceiling
of the Planetarium

My mom is helping
me pack and I can feel her thinking
that this is my first step to leaving
her behind—she keeps sighing
heavily, like she is picturing
the *saddest* things in the world.

I know it wasn't easy, having
me so young, raising
me alone, putting
her dreams on hold, forgetting
about things she'd been wanting
to do forever, like dancing
on Broadway, singing
in musicals, taking
on the world like I am about to.

I can't imagine *anything* stopping
me from living
the kind of life I want.

And when we're in the workshops, learning
about ways to make a difference, sharing
ideas with other kids, I know I'll be thinking
about my mom, working
at a job she doesn't really like, giving
me *so much*.

Whatever I end up doing
it will have meaning
because of her.

I won't leave without telling
her that.

On the Bus
Christopher

Packing for New York
I picture this:

Greyhound rolling
down the highway
in the middle of the night.

Through the mountains
climbing, falling
in the path of high-beam light.

In the window
we're reflected,
touching, talking, sleeping tight.

MY YELLOW MINI

Mark

Is bright as the sun,
speedy and slick.

It takes me places I need to go,
determined and quick.

Maybe it's true that my dad wouldn't have wanted me
to buy it. Maybe he would've seen it

As a ticking time bomb, like the one that landed
on his roof as a kid.

But I don't believe that—not now that it helped me
find the land he loved. Now,

If he's looking down, he'll see me and Mary
winding up the mountain.

He'll hear me humming Chopin
and he'll know that I'm okay.